THE
TOOTH FAIRY'S
RULES

THE TOOTH FAIRY'S RULES

Leena R. Reichel

gatekeeper press

Columbus, Ohio

The Tooth Fairy's Rules

Published by Gatekeeper Press
2167 Stringtown Rd, Suite 109
Columbus, OH 43123-2989
www.GatekeeperPress.com

The cover design, interior formatting, typesetting, and editorial work for this book are entirely the product of the author. Gatekeeper Press did not participate in and is not responsible for any aspect of these elements.

Library of Congress Control Number: 2020949166

ISBN (hardcover): 9781662913570

When you lose a tooth, it's exciting to know

That the Tooth Fairy will leave money under your pillow.

But before this is a guarantee,

She has some rules, so listen to me.

Let's learn what the Tooth Fairy has to say

About cleaning your teeth twice a day.

Make sure you brush and floss morning and night,

When you wake up for school and before you turn out the light.

She comes to kids' homes who brush for two minutes long.

To make sure you're brushing long enough, set a timer or play a song.

Brush all around your mouth, spending time on each tooth.

Brush the front, the back, and the chewing surface too.

6

When you're brushing your teeth, lightly brush your tongue too,

Because a squeaky-clean tongue is healthy for you.

It's time to switch your toothbrush when the bristles start to flare.

This usually happens three or four times a year.

Always remember not to swallow your toothpaste,

Even if you really love the taste.

Swallowing your toothpaste isn't funny –

It's meant for your teeth and not your tummy.

10

Flossing your teeth is good for you too,

So make it a habit because it's healthy to do.

To floss, put the string between your teeth and move it side to side.

Flossing is very important because this is where germs like to hide.

12

Rinse off the floss before you move to each part

Because moving the germs from one tooth to another wouldn't be very smart.

Sometimes it's hard to do this by yourself,

So don't be afraid to ask a grown-up for help.

A grown-up can help you keep your teeth clean.

Sometimes it takes teamwork to practice good hygiene.

When your teeth aren't clean, your gums may look red.

If you clean them well, they'll look healthy instead.

When your adult teeth grow in, make sure you take good care.

Treat them well because you won't get another pair.

So, make sure to follow these rules when you floss and brush.

Spend enough time and try not to rush.

18

If you brush too quickly and don't clean very well,
You'll have germs in your mouth and your breath will start to smell.

Keeping your mouth clean is good for your whole body,
So let's make brushing and flossing your new favorite hobby.

The Tooth Fairy and dentist speak every day,

So make sure your dentist only has only good things to say.

If you follow these rules and keep them up, too,

The Tooth Fairy and dentist will be so proud of you.

Looking back, you'll be happy you learned this when you were young
Because needing dentures isn't very fun.

When you lose a tooth, remember these things,
And you'll see how much money the Tooth Fairy brings.

24

CPSIA information can be obtained
at www.ICGtesting.com
Printed in the USA
LVRC091439110621
690001LV00008B/454

9 781662 913570